Making Friends with Samson

ALISON PETERS

Illustrated by Nathan Jurevicius

sundance
A Haights Cross Communications Company

The Story Characters

Nathan
He really wants
a dog.

Mike and his pals
They're trouble.

Mom and Dad
They mean well.

The Story Setting

TABLE OF CONTENTS

Nathan's Wish List

Nathan Clark had always wanted a dog. When his family moved to the city, it was all he could think about.

"We don't have a backyard," said Mom.

"The city's no place for a dog," said Dad.

Nathan dreamed that one day they would change their minds. When they did, he would be ready.

Nathan read books about dogs. He knew what to feed them. He knew what to do if they had fleas. He knew exactly what he would do with his very own dog.

In his top drawer was his list.

Great Things to Do with a Dog

1. Take the dog everywhere, like fishing and to Uncle Bill's farm.
2. Teach it to sit.
3. Teach it to wait at the door for me.
4. Let it sleep beside my bed.

After a few days at his new school, Nathan added two things to his list.

5. Teach it to fetch things like newspapers, sticks, and baseball hats—after Mike's pals take them.
6. Teach it to scare off other dogs, like Mike's dog, Monster.

Nathan had even picked out a name for his dog—Samson.

Nathan's Birthday

On his birthday, Mom and Dad put a big box on his bed.

"Happy Birthday, Nathan," said Mom.

Pete's Pets was written on the side of
the box. And there were holes along
the top so that a puppy could breathe.

"You'll be surprised," Dad smiled.

Nathan knew what it was. He held in an excited squeal as he opened the top of the box.

He couldn't wait to meet his new,
furry, friendly, jumping, barking,
tail-wagging . . .

BIRD?! His dog was a bird! It couldn't bark or jump or wag its tail. In fact, it didn't move at all. For a second, it didn't seem real.

"Oh," Nathan gulped. "It . . . it sure is a surprise."

It was worse than the surprise he got
on his last birthday. Nathan had
wanted a special new computer game.
Instead, he found a book about boats
on the end of his bed.

CHAPTER ③

Chirp! Chirp!

For weeks, the bird sat silently staring at him. Nathan changed the bird's water and seed every few days. But he didn't speak to it. What was the point?

Whenever Nathan walked near the cage, the bird moved as far away from him as it could.

One day, the bird tilted its head to
one side and made a small sound.
"Chirp," it squeaked.

"Was that you, bird?" Nathan asked.

"Chirp," the bird sang, then turned
upside down and spread its wings.

"So you can hang upside down. So what? You can't chase a stick or catch a ball. What good are you?" Nathan grumbled.

The next time Nathan came near the cage, the bird didn't move away.

Nathan moved closer. The bird didn't
move. Nathan put his hand inside the
cage. The bird still didn't move.
Nathan tried to grab the bird. It bit
him hard.

"BIRRDD!!!!" Nathan yelled, "You nearly bit off my finger!"

Frightened, the bird flapped inside the cage. Its wings crashed against the bars.

"Shhh," Nathan whispered, "Sorry, bird. It's okay. Shhh."

Slowly the bird calmed down.

CHAPTER 4

Making Friends with Bird

A few days later, Nathan tried again. Carefully he stuck his finger inside the cage. The bird didn't move. Nathan put his finger near the perch. The bird HOPPED ON!

"Good bird," he whispered. "Good bird."

Every afternoon they practiced, over and over and over again.

Soon Nathan could even take the bird out of the cage. One night, the bird flew onto Nathan's head, and he wore the bird to dinner.

"You couldn't do that with a dog!" said Dad.

"I suppose," Nathan shrugged. He still knew a dog would be better than a bird.

At school the next day, all Nathan could think about was the bird.

"What can I teach it next?" he
wondered. He kept thinking as he ate
his sandwich and watched the boys
playing baseball.

Just then, Mike and his pals crept up.

"Got it!" yelled Mike, as he swiped the hat from Nathan's head. It was his favorite hat—the old blue one that Uncle Bill had given him. Mike walked away with Nathan's hat.

Nathan sat in the library for the rest of the lunch break. Mike and his pals never went in there.

As Nathan looked through the
magazines, he couldn't believe his
eyes. On one cover, there was a
photograph of a man. He was wearing
black leather and riding a motorcycle.
A bird sat on the handlebars.

It was trained to stay there while the motorcycle sped along!

Nathan had an idea.

...iding Lessons

After school, Nathan went down to the basement with the birdcage. He took out the bird, and he put it on the handlebars of his bike.

He slowly rode the bike in a circle.
Then he rode faster. The bird held on!

The next day, Nathan put the bird on his bike and rode behind his apartment building. The bird didn't fly away.

Nathan rode the bike in a circle, faster and faster. Still the bird held on. It was incredible!

Nathan was excited. He couldn't wait to show somebody. But who? Dad was working overtime at the hardware store. Mom was working at the cafe.

Nathan thought about Mike and his
pals. The bird needed more practice.
But it would be cool to show off their
new trick. Nathan opened the gate and
took the bird to the park.

CHAPTER  6

Mike and Monster

Mike and his pals were playing ball.
Their bikes were by a tree. Monster and
the other dogs were on guard duty.

Nathan rode his bike slowly along the path. Maybe they'd notice. Maybe they would want to come and have a look. Maybe they'd be impressed. They might even let him play!

Monster saw the bird first.

"Grrrrrrrr." The boys looked up.
Monster pulled at his leash. The other
dogs barked. The bird froze in fear.

"Oh no," whispered Nathan.

"No hat today, Nathan?" Mike asked.
The boys laughed.

"Is that a plastic tweetie bird on your handlebars?" Mike teased.

The bird began to flap its wings.

"Ooooh, it moves! HELLO, TWEETIE," Mike yelled, as he grabbed at the bird.

The bird flew off the handlebars in
panic. It soared past the tree and out
of sight. Monster and the other dogs
went wild.

Mike and his pals laughed, but Nathan hardly heard them. He pedaled past the boys, past the tree, past the dogs, and into the woods behind the park.

"I wish I never left the basement," he said to himself. He rode along, searching for his bird in the trees. It was no good. The bird was gone.

CHAPTER 7

Bird in Danger

Slowly Nathan pedaled back to the park. Mike and his pals were playing ball again.

Monster and the other dogs were quiet
now. Just then the dogs' ears shot up.

"Chirp! Chirp! Chirrrrup!" There was
his bird, perched on a low branch. The
dogs snapped at its tail feathers.

"Psst, bird," Nathan called desperately. "Come on, bird."

But the bird wouldn't go to Nathan. It screeched and flew onto the seat of a bike. The dogs were a barking tangle of leashes, tails, and teeth.

The bird flew to another bike seat and then another. Finally it landed on Mike's bike, which was propped against the tree. Uncle Bill's blue hat was hanging from the brake handle.

Monster growled and jumped over the other dogs with his jaws snapping. His leash was stretched tight.

"Oh no! He'll bite my bird for sure," Nathan cried.

Mike ran toward the tree. Suddenly there was a yelp and a yell, as he tripped over Monster's leash. Mike flew through the air and fell on his bike. Monster landed on top. What a mess!

The other boys began to laugh.
Monster licked Mike's face. "Get off,
you stupid dog!" Mike yelled.

The bird landed on Mike's head and
screeched loudly. The boys laughed
harder, but not as hard as Nathan.

"That's a cool bird," said one of the boys. "How did you train it?"

"It takes practice—and a smart bird!" Nathan said. Then he grabbed his hat off of Mike's bike.

"Can you train dogs?" the boy asked.

"Probably," Nathan smiled. "But I like birds better."

That night, Nathan moved the cage
so that it was next to his bed.

"Hey, bird," Nathan said softly. "You
need a real name."

"From now on your name is Samson. Goodnight, Samson," Nathan said.

Samson shook himself, ruffled his feathers, and tucked his head under his wing.

GLOSSARY

desperately

in a nervous or
fearful way

impressed

thought something was great

incredible

very hard to believe

panic

great fear

perched
sitting still like a bird
on a branch

propped
leaned up against
something

ruffled
made his feathers puff up

searching
looking very hard

Talking with the Author and the Illustrator

Alison Peters (author)

Who is your favorite cartoon character?
  Bart Simpson.

If you could go anywhere, where would it be?
  Once I swam with two whales off the coast of
  Patagonia—I'd go back there in a flash.

What are three things that you can't live without?
  Oxygen, sleep, and my glasses.

Nathan Jurevicius (illustrator)

What is your favorite breakfast?
  Sliced banana on cereal and green tea.

Who is your favorite cartoon character?
  Felix the Cat.

What are three things that you can't live without?
  I can't live without air, love, and hope.

Published by Sundance Publishing
P.O. Box 1326, 234 Taylor Street, Littleton, MA 01460
800-343-8204

First published 1999 as Sparklers by
Blake Education, Locked Bag 2022, Glebe 2037, Australia
Exclusive United States Distribution: Sundance Publishing

ISBN 0-7608-5141-7

Printed in Canada